The Little P in the Forest

THe NeeNY HAIReD FAMILY

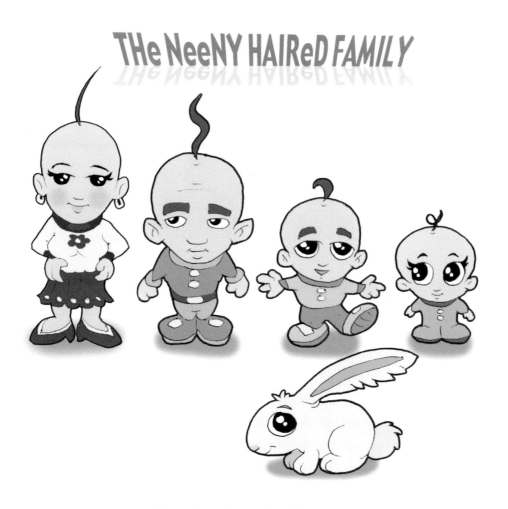

By: Doris Wright Garrett

The Little People in the Forest

By: Doris Wright Garrett
Illustrations by: Frank Sudol

To order additional copies of this book, contact:
Xlibris Corporation
1-888-795-4274
www.Xlibris.com
Orders@Xlibris.com

Dedication

This story was inspired by Vanessa, Roger Jr. and Leanne Garrett and is dedicated to Roger Garrett Sr,

The Little People in the Forest

Foreward

The Little People in the Forest is a fictitious story written for young children. In this story, other forest people are mentioned, but not shown in the illustrations for the sole purpose that each child reading this can then use his or her imagination as to how they looked.

I think it would be a great experience for friends to get together and tell each other how they pictured the other forest people.

I hope each child reads and enjoys this little book.

Once upon a time in a dark green forest, far away from all the other forest people, there lived the tiniest family of forest people anywhere. There was Poppa Albert Hair, Momma Ruth Hair, Big Brother Billy Hair, and Baby Susan Hair. This family was called the Neeny Hair family. You see, they did not always live in the dark part of the green forest, but because they were different from everyone else, the mean old forest people made them leave the bright edge of the forest and live in darkness. The other forest people would look at them and laugh saying, "Look at the teeny, neeny hair on their head. They are the Neeny hair family! They can't live out here in the forest with us! They have to live way back in the dark part of the green forest by themselves!" The bigger forest people laughed and went on their way.

This story is about the tiniest Neeny Hair Family. You see, they were all different because each one had only one teeny neeny strand of hair, which grew straight out from the top of their head. The Neeny Hair family also had skin color like no one else in the forest. The color of their skin glowed like colors of every nation. If they gave a light tap on the edge of their nose, they would glow really bright.

The Neeny Hair family also had a tiny pet bunny that only had one long ear. He was named Apache, because he looked like an Indian with a feather sticking out of his head. Because he was different, the other bunnies in the forest would not play with him and chased him also into the dark green forest. This is where the Neeny Hair family found him and took him to live with them as their pet.

The Neeny Hair family did not like living in the dark green forest all the time. Momma Ruth Hair and Poppa Albert Hair wanted friends to talk with and other children to play with their children. "We must find a place to build our perfect home," said Momma Ruth Hair. "We cannot stay here. It is too close to the tall forest people and I'm afraid they might do something bad to us one night while we are sleep."

Poppa Albert said, "I've been looking around, but just can't find a safe place for us. Maybe tomorrow will be better."

Even though the Neeny Hair family was laughed at and sometimes frightened by the forest people, they never stopped smiling.

They were a very happy and loving family. The next morning as usual, the Neeny Hair family gathered their belongings and took off to find a new shelter.

After walking for hours, Poppa Albert noticed Apache running back and forth, sitting on his hind legs and wiggling his one long ear. "What is it?" he asked and walked in the direction of the bunny.

Apache had found a huge, hollowed out tree stump that would protect the Neeny Hair family and himself from the wind and rain.

Poppa Albert called to his family to come, "Look!" he said, "Apache has found us a place to rest for the night."

Big Brother Billy Hair hugged Apache and said, "He is the smartest bunny in the whole world!"

Baby Susan Hair answered, "I am glad he is our bunny."

Momma Ruth thought to herself it wasn't the perfect place to live forever, but it was far enough away from the mean forest people so that they felt safe and it would certainly protect them through the night. Once they were settled down in the tree stump, a temporary home for that night, Baby Susan Hair asked Momma Ruth, "Why did all the other forest people make fun of us and make us leave our home, Momma?"

Momma Ruth Hair replied, "Baby Susan, some people are frightened when they come across people that are different from them and rather than trying to become friends, they just don't want to be bothered and will call you names or run you off away from them. Remember what Poppa told us, we are all loved by God – we are just the lucky ones He chose to be different from the rest."

Big Brother Billy Hair added, "Even though the mean forest people made us leave our home, we are still a happy family and we love each other. Our skin shines like a golden flashlight in the dark. Our glowing skin helped us find berries to eat and leaves to keep us warm."

Poppa had to chime in saying, "Baby Susan, how many people have a fine bunny like our Apache? He found this tree stump for us in the forest. We would not have ventured out this way if it wasn't for him."

Apache sensed they were praising him so he sat up on his hind legs, wiggled his one long ear, made his little bunny noise, and curled up and went to sleep in his corner of the tree stump.

"Will we have to live in the tree stump forever?" asked Baby Susan.

"No!" said Momma Ruth. "One day, we will find a place to call our home. It will be the perfect place to live."

"Well," said Poppa Albert, "We did enough chatting. We must go now to look for food to eat for our supper."

The Neeny Hair family held each other's hands and walked through the forest, looking for nuts and berries. It was a long night and the Neeny Hair family still had not found any food.

"I'm hungry," said Baby Susan.

"So am I," said Big Brother Billy.

Poppa Albert and Momma Ruth looked at each other, and although they were tired and hungry, and quite sad inside, they just smiled and Momma Ruth said out loud, "Hey, did we not eat a nice meal of nuts for breakfast and berries for lunch that we gathered before we left for the dark green forest?"

"Yes," the children replied.

"Well," said Momma Ruth, as they headed back to their tree stump home for the night. "When we go to sleep and close our eyes, just think of those beautiful meals and how our tummies were so full, it will take our minds off eating. In fact, I'm getting full just talking about it."

Baby Susan and Big Brother Billy laughed and said, "So am I Momma, so am I!"

"Tomorrow," Poppa Albert said, "Will be a better day." "Poppa Albert knew Momma Ruth always had a way of making not just the children, but he himself forget their problems, at least for the moment.

So the Neeny Hair family went inside the big hole in the tree stump, kissed each other good night, said a prayer, and went to sleep.

Momma Ruth closed her eyes, but deep down she was hoping her prayer of finding food and a place to live would be answered soon. She was still praying that one day they would meet a family with children to play with Baby Susan and Brother Billy and that she and Poppa would also have friends.

Early the next morning, Poppa Albert was awakened with the sound of something or someone smacking their lips. He looked around, but the rest of the family was still asleep. "What is that noise?" Poppa Albert wondered. He stretched and got up. He stuck his head out of the opening in the tree stump only to see, Apache, the bunny chewing something red and making quite a sound. Poppa Albert walked over to the rabbit, bent down to see what he had, and low and behold, it was a red wild strawberry!

"Momma Ruth!" Poppa Albert called, "Children, wake up! Apache knows where to find us food!"

The family woke up fast on the word food and ran outside. Poppa Albert said to Apache, "Take us to the berries you found."

Now, Apache, being a smart bunny knew just what Poppa Albert meant. The family gathered their belongings because they had no intentions of staying there another night. They must find a place to build a house.

Apache hopped and ran in front of the Neeny Hair family and after a long tiring walk they came to a berry bush. The Neeny Hair family was so happy to get something to eat that they picked and ate until their little tummies were full. The Neeny Hair family did not notice until they were ready to gather berries for their supper that the other side of the bush was picked clean, as if someone else had been there ahead of them. Momma Ruth and Poppa Albert looked at each other and wondered who else could be in the forest with them. Poppa said, "Not to worry Momma. They probably ate and left." So, Momma Ruth filled her little basket to the brim with berries.

"We must leave now children," said Poppa Albert, "We will look for more food on our way."

Big Brother Billy said, "It's a good thing that our skin glows so brightly or we would no be able to see in this dark green forest."

The Neeny Hair family gathered their belongings and off they went, hoping that soon they would find a place for their perfect home. While the Neeny Hair family walked and walked, they looked for nuts and berries that would feed them in the morning. The tiny basket, even completely filled, would only be enough food for the family for one meal that night. Momma Ruth thought, "Oh dear! Another morning for the family to go hungry. Maybe, if I can get them to bed early, with the children still full from supper, they will not have time to think of food in the morning. We will get right up and get an early start."

Just at that moment a voice called, "Hello! Hello! You there with the flashlight, would you help me?"

Poppa Albert walked closer to the voice staying close to a fallen tree so he would stay out of sight. "Who can this be?" he wondered.

Poppa Albert walked a few steps more and by the glow of his skin, he saw it was the lumberjack they used to see walking past the edge of the forest where they used to live. The lumberjack never saw them or the other forest people because they would run and hide even though he looked friendly. The lumberjack asked, "Can you help me?" as he came and sat down on a log.

After his eyes got used to the glow from the little family, he looked at the Neeny Hair family in surprise. "What is this?" he asked. "You're the light I saw. I thought you were another lumberjack. I've never seen such a tiny family! And certainly not one that glows!"

To the amazement of the Neeny Hair family, that was all he said. He never made fun of their one strand of hair, their size, or their glowing skin. The lumberjack explained how he had to mark some trees that were to be cut down in the dark green forest, and after a while, he sat down to eat lunch and he fell asleep. "My flashlight must have rolled somewhere and I could not find it. Then I thought your light was another lumberjack."

The Neeny Hair family had seen what a kind man he was. "We will be glad to help you," said Poppa Albert. "Our glowing skin will throw the light."

The Neeny Hair family pressed their fingers to their nose and threw a ray of light around the trees. After looking and looking, they finally found the lumberjack's flashlight.

Poppa Albert explained how they must leave the forest and find a place to live. The lumberjack wished them good luck and told them, "Do not go the way I came in. It's filled with marsh and tall grasses and your family would surely drown. If you head straight, I'm pretty sure it's safe."

The lumberjack really appreciated their help, waved and went on his way. The Neeny Hair family watched him until he faded out of sight.

"Put the light out! Put the light out!" shouted a voice from way up high.

Poppa Albert and Momma Ruth looked up and saw it was Mrs. Bat and her family.

"Oh, we are so sorry!" they said as the family touched their nose and dimmed the glow. "I see you and your family are out getting your supper for the night."

"Yes," said Mrs. Bat, "We eat at night and sleep in the day. Well, good-bye. Thank you and good night!" The bat family flew higher into the dark trees looking for their meal.

"They won't be hungry," Momma Ruth said sadly to herself. Then Momma Ruth said, "I think we've had a busy day and we should turn in early so we can get an early start in the morning. We can rest up against this log and use some leaves to cover us."

Big Brother Billy was getting smart. He knew they had no food and Momma Ruth was trying to get their minds off of it. He would be strong for them and Baby Susan and go along with bedding down early.

The next morning Poppa Albert called to the family to wake up. "We must really travel today. We want to find a place to build our home before the winter comes."

Baby Susan jumped up and asked Momma Ruth, "Are we going to eat first? I'm hungry!"

Big Brother Billy Hair said, "Wouldn't you like to eat with me later on Baby Susan? This way we can see what is ahead of us faster."

Baby Susan loved doing things with her big brother and squealed, "Yes, yes!"

So off they went.

Momma Ruth and Poppa Albert smiled proudly at their son. The Neeny Hair family really walked far this time and they did not stop for anything. Yes, they were tired and quite hungry, but after some time they noticed the forest trees were thinning out and it didn't seem quite as dark. Did this mean they had found a clearing that might be warm and bright?

Poppa Albert was getting excited now and said, "Hurry! Family, lets see what is at the end of this trail!"

While walking, Big Brother Billy thought he saw another rabbit running through the forest, but being dark, it could have been his shadow from the glow. It seemed quite larger than Apache. At the same time, Apache was standing up wiggling his ear and nose and all of a sudden he took off into the woods in the direction of what Big Brother Billy thought was a rabbit.

Big Brother Billy yelled, "Apache ran off chasing something that looked like another rabbit. I must go after him."

"Not alone," said Poppa Albert. "We will all go together." So the whole family took off after their pet Apache.

As they were running, the trees seemed to thin out and they could also hear singing. It was getting brighter as they ran. Berry bushes, wild mushrooms, and hazel nuts seemed to grow up and down this path. Momma Ruth said, "If this isn't as close to a perfect place to live, I don't know what is."

When they reached the end of the forest, Momma Ruth and Poppa Albert could not believe their eyes. Here, right in front of them there was another tiny family just like them. They had one hair sticking out from the top of their head and their skin was glowing so brightly it looked like a rainbow of colors.

"Could this be some of our relatives that Grand-Mom Harriet used to speak of before she passed away?" said Brother Billy. "Grand-Mom used to say because our family was different it seemed we were all scattered away because others did not want us around."

Momma Ruth and Poppa Albert could not stop smiling because they were thinking the same thing. This had to be their lost family.

Baby Susan pulled on Momma Ruth's dress and said, "What about Apache? Where is he?" She was not worried about the other people. She was more interested in finding her pet bunny.

Poppa Albert said, "Your right Baby Susan." Taking one last look at the tiny singing family, he called in a soft voice, "Apache!

Apache! Where are you?" But, his voice was not soft enough because all of a sudden, the singing stopped. This frightened the Neeny Hair family just a little and they started to run back into the woods.

"Wait!" said a soft kind voice. "Please don't go!"

Poppa and Momma gathered their children close to them. The Tiny Hair family came toward them. The Father spoke and said, "We are the Hair family. My name is Jeff, my wife is June, and these are our children Jess and Elaine. Along time ago, we used to live at the other end of this forest, but because of our height and skin color, the mean forest people called us weirdoes and made us leave. We found our way here after a time and now live safely away from the mean forest people where it is nice and bright."

The Neeny Hair family could not believe they had found family and friends in the same area. This was truly a happy day.

"Please stay, "said June Hair, "Stay here in the meadows with us. There are plenty of berries, nuts, and mushrooms and we have a garden of vegetables that we plant and share. We will help you build your house in any spot you wish."

Momma Ruth was already picturing her new little home. It would be made out of small branches and big wide green leaves with logs and mud to hold it together. There would be a fine front porch with steps that would sparkle like stars from tiny pieces of glass that would be mixed in their mud. Poppa Albert had found the glass as they walked through the forest.

Just then, Baby Susan Hair said in an excited voice, "Look Poppa! There is Apache sitting in front of that house with another rabbit."

Apache seemed to be quite content with his new friends. In his mind he was saying, "Oh how I wish this could be our new home. I finally have a friend to run around and play with."

Apache did not know yet that Momma Ruth and Poppa Albert were already planning that this was their perfect place to live. "This has been the happiest day ever," said Momma Ruth to her family. "We found the perfect place to live, new friends for Poppa and I, and playmates for our children. All my prayers have been answered."

They all gave a hug, gathered their belongings and walked out of the dark green forest forever toward the meadow and the beautiful flowers and warm sunshine.

A Happy Ending

CPSIA information can be obtained
at www.ICGtesting.com
Printed in the USA
LVIC06n1932260517
536019LV00006B/11

*9 7 8 1 4 2 5 7 5 5 0 5 8 *